ABRACADABRA to ZIGZAG

AN ALPHABET BOOK!

WORDS BY NANCY LECOURT

PICTURES BY BARBARA LEHMAN

TICKETS

LOTHROP, LEE & SHEPARD BOOKS • NEW YORK

Library of Congress Cataloging in Publication Data. Lecourt, Nancy. Abracadabra—zigzag / by Nancy Lecourt ; illustrations by Barbara Lehman.   p.   cm. Summary: An alphabet book introducing such words as bigwig, licketysplit, mishmash, and shillyshally. ISBN 0-688-09481-3.   —ISBN 0-688-09482-1 (lib. bdg.)   [1. Alphabet.] I. Lehman, Barbara, ill. II. Title. PZ7.L488Ab 1990 [E]—dc20   89-12879 CIP AC

Aa

abracadabra

Bb

bigwig

Cc

creepy crawly

Dd

dillydally

Ee

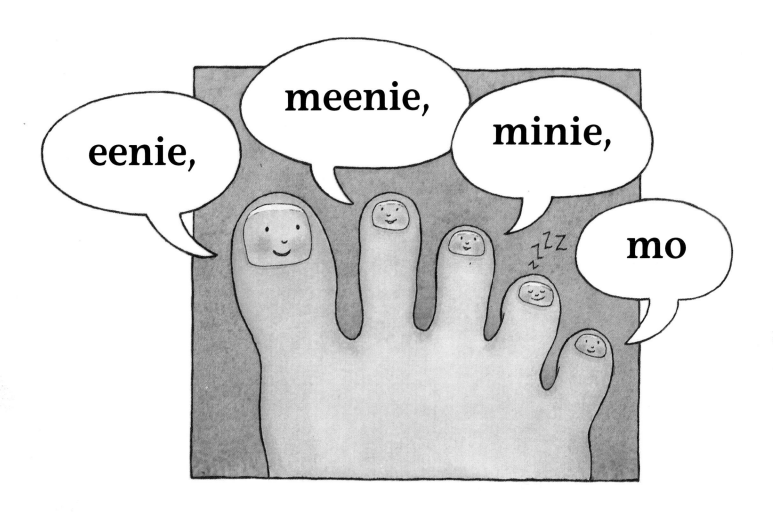

Ff

flip-flop

Gg

gewgaw

hurdy-gurdy

Ii

itsy bitsy

Jj

jeepers creepers

Kk

knickerbockers

Ll

licketysplit

Mm

mishmash

Nn

nip and tuck

Oo

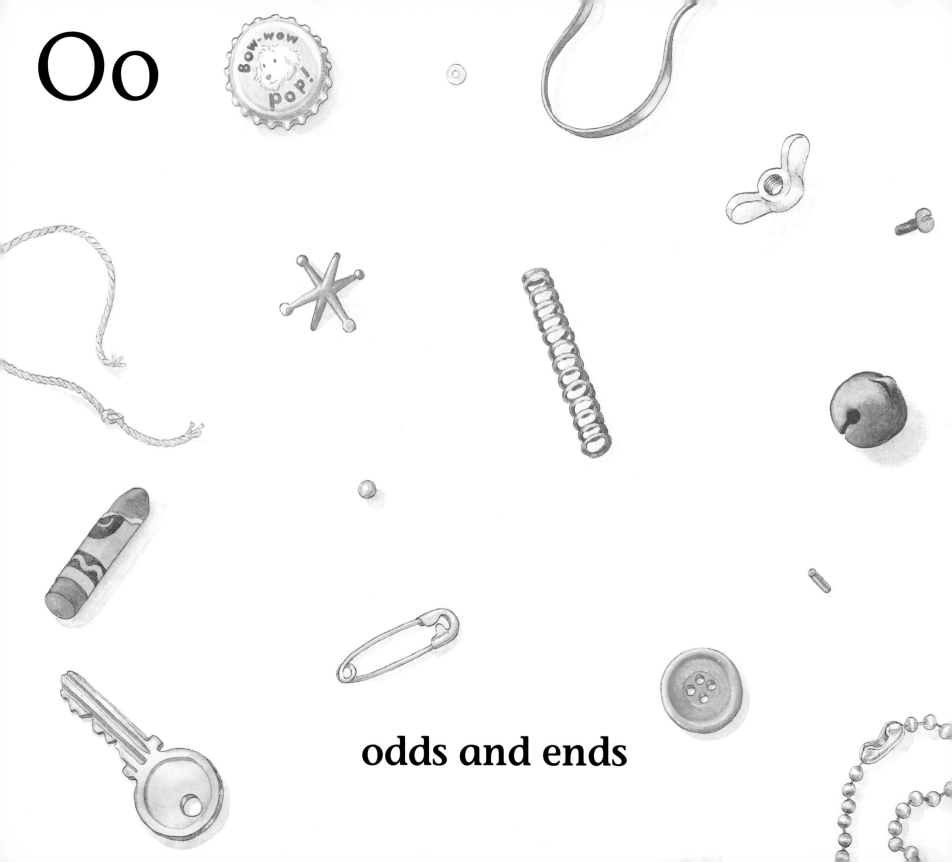

odds and ends

Pp

pitter-patter

Qq

quackety quack

Rr

rolypoly

shipshape

Tt

topsy-turvy

Uu

upsy daisy

Vv

va-va-va-VOOM

Ww

wigwam

Xx

Xianggang

Yy

yoo-hoo!

Zz

zigzag

GLOSSARY

Words change over time, and new words are always being invented. Some of the words in this book, such as dillydally, were invented by simply changing the vowel of a word to make a rhyme. Others, such as bigwig, have more to do with their meanings than with their sounds. Still others are so old or obscure that no one is quite sure how they came to be.

abracadabra a charm or spell. Long ago this word was used to ask the gods for help when performing magic.

bigwig an important person. Louis the 14th of France set the style of wearing long, flowing wigs; the more important the person, the bigger the wig.

creepy crawly a creeping or crawling animal, especially an insect. This expression was first used in 1855 and comes from the word *creepy*, meaning the feeling of something crawling on the skin.

dillydally to spend time idly. This word started with an ancient French word for "chat" that sounded like dally.

eenie, meenie, minie, mo a choosing rhyme. This rhyme was first used by Druid priests in ancient Great Britain and France.

flip-flop a turnaround; also a backward somersault. This word started out as just plain "flip," which means "toss," and came into use around 1655.

gewgaw a fancy thing that has little value. No one knows where this word came from.

hurdy-gurdy a barrel organ. The first hurdy-gurdys had both strings and keys and were very loud. The name comes from the English word *hirdy girdy*, which meant uproar.

itsy bitsy small, tiny. A rhyming variation of "little bit," used in the U.S. since the late 1800s.

jeepers creepers a mild exclamation of surprise. The phrase comes from *jeepers*, a polite way to swear by Jesus, and was first used in the U.S. in 1925.

knickerbockers short trousers gathered at the knee. From Diedrich Knickerbocker, the pen name Washington Irving used for his humorous history of New York that included illustrations of Dutchmen wearing knickers.

licketysplit going at a fast pace. First used in the U.S. in the mid-1800s, it was then considered a very elegant phrase.

mishmash a mixture, a hodgepodge. This word started out in England in the 1500s.

nip and tuck a race in which the lead keeps changing. First used in the U.S. about 1832, the phrase comes from combining "to nip someone out," which meant to beat someone, and "tuck," which meant vigor.

odds and ends an assortment of miscellaneous things. This phrase dates from the 1746 English "odd end," meaning the leftover piece of a set.

pitter-patter gently beating sounds. No one is certain where this word came from, but some think it began with the medieval English word for the sounds of a babbled prayer.

quackety quack the sound a duck makes. The origin of this phrase is unknown.

rolypoly round, stout; a rolled pastry filled with jam. This word started out in Great Britain. It may have come from *rowly-powly*, which meant a worthless fellow, or from *rouly-pouly*, which was a bowling game.

shipshape neat, orderly. This English term from the 1630s refers to the way things are arranged on a ship, secure and neat in a small space.

topsy-turvy with the top where the bottom should be. This word comes from the medieval phrase *top syd turvye* for top side down.

upsy daisy an exclamation used when lifting a child. In use from 1860, this may be a variation of the phrase *lack-a-day*.

va-va-va-voom a roaring sound, like the revving of a motor, expressing excitement. This word was first used in the U.S. in the 1960s.

wigwam Native American word for cabin, tent, or hut. This comes from the Algonquin word *wikiwam*, meaning house.

Xianggang This is the way Hong Kong is spelled in the Pinyin writing system. Pinyin is a way of writing Chinese in the English alphabet.

yoo-hoo an exclamation used to call attention. In medieval English, "yo" was used to answer to a roll call.

zigzag a line with frequent sharp turns from side to side. It comes from the German word *zickzack* and was first used to describe the barriers built around a fort to defend it.